Mauritius

by Theresa Rebeck

A SAMUEL FRENCH ACTING EDITION

SAMUEL FRENCH

FOUNDED 1830

NEW YORK HOLLYWOOD LONDON TORONTO

SAMUELFRENCH.COM

ISBN 978-0-573-66019-1   Printed in U.S.A.   #14837

IMPORTANT BILLING AND CREDIT REQUIREMENTS

MAURITIUS had its world premier at the Boston Center for the Arts on October 6th, 2006. The production was directed by Rebecca Bayla Taichman with set design by Eugene Lee. Miranda Hoffman was the costume designer, Paul Whitaker was the lighting designer, and Martin Desjardins was both sound designer and composer. Rick Sordelet served as the production's fight director. The production stage manager was Stephen Kaus with assistant stage manager, Maureen Lane. The cast was as follows:

JACKIE	Marin Ireland
PHILIP	Robert Dorfman
DENNIS	Michael Aronov
STERLING	James Gale
MARY	Laura Latreille

MAURITIUS had its world New York premier at the Biltmore Theatre on October 4th, 2007. The production was directed by Doug Hughes with set design by John Lee Beatty, lighting design by Paul Gallo, costume design by Catherine Zuber, original music and sound design by David Van Tieghem. The Stage Manager was Elizabeth Moloney. The cast was as follows:

JACKIE	Alison Pill
PHILIP	Dylan Baker
DENNIS	Bobby Cannavale
STERLING	F. Murray Abraham
MARY	Katie Finneran

CHARACTERS

JACKIE
PHILIP
DENNIS
STERLING
MARY

ACT 1

Scene 1

(*A shop.* **JACKIE** *stands in light, holding a book.* **PHILIP** *at the counter, reading a book. There is someone in the corner of the room, reading a newspaper.*)

JACKIE. Can you, excuse me, I was wondering, I need someone to look at this. I'm not sure what it is. It's quite old, and my understanding is that it could be, you know, someone told me that it was maybe worth a lot of money. I don't actually, I mean, it's mine, it is mine, but I don't know a lot about it.

(*Ignoring her,* **PHILIP** *picks his nose.*)

So they said that you could maybe look at it, that you have some expertise in this area and that actually you're really knowledgeable and you would be the person to ask.

(*beat*)

It's stamps.

(*She opens the book, to show him.*)

I know a lot of people collect stamps, I never did, but I know that it is a popular hobby with some people. Not just nerds, either, normal – oh. Sorry. Sorry.

(*beat*)

It's mine to sell, though. I mean, I do own it. It's been in our family for a long time, there's some, in there, eighteen-something. Which, I have no idea if they're real, I guess they could be fake. With my luck they probably are fake, but I'm trying not to, I'm trying, actually, to be positive, although I actually don't judge myself for

7

being negative more or less most of the time. Not that I'm defending negativity. And it's not like I think the stamps are fake, either. I don't think they are. They're real. No question. At all. That's so.... Anyway.

(*She nods. A beat.*)

PHILIP. Why do you think that?

JACKIE. What? Oh. Sorry. Sorry! What?

PHILIP. You said you don't think the stamps are forgeries, but you also admit that you don't know anything about stamps. So what makes you think your stamps are authentic?

JACKIE. I don't, uh –

PHILIP. Does this look like Antiques Roadshow to you? Do you want to be on television?

JACKIE. No, no, of course, I –

PHILIP. Do I know you?

JACKIE. No, But they –

PHILIP. They, they who?

JACKIE. Who?

PHILIP. Yes, "who?"

JACKIE. Well, you know, people –

PHILIP. People, what people?

JACKIE. (*flustered*) I talked to this person, this person, in this store –

PHILIP. You talked to a person in a store?

JACKIE. Yes, who said –

PHILIP. But you don't know who this person is?

JACKIE. Yes! I mean, I don't know his name.

PHILIP. Ah, that person!

(*The newspaper shifts. In the corner,* **DENNIS** *appears from behind the paper. He watches.*)

JACKIE. Okay. Could you –

PHILIP. Could I what? I'm working here. Do I know you?

JACKIE. This guy, in this store –

PHILIP. What store?

JACKIE. It was, I was there buying something else. And they were also, it was also a a, stamp store, and...

PHILIP. A stamp store.

JACKIE. Yes, it was for stamps and things like comic books, and, and Yugioh cards...

PHILIP. Is that what you were buying? Yugioh cards?

JACKIE. No. I was buying... a comic book.

(*She fades, depressed now.*)

PHILIP. Ah.

JACKIE. He's always, really, pretty nice to me. He said to call you.

PHILIP. The nice person in the Yugioh store said he would not look at your stamps, is that what he said?

JACKIE. He said –

PHILIP. It doesn't matter what he said. I will not look at your stamps, either.

JACKIE. Okay. Sure, okay.

(*beat*)

I mean, I just –

PHILIP. Thank you.

(*A beat.*)

JACKIE. (*a small flare of anger*) Okay, fine. That's fine, I don't. You know, these things are worth a lot. They are like, a treasure, they're like – you know. I'm just telling you. Okay?

PHILIP. If you know what they're worth, then why are you asking me?

JACKIE. Because I... need help.

(*She stands there for a moment, suddenly fighting back tears.* **PHILIP** *stares at her. She takes back her book.*)

DENNIS. I'll look at it.

JACKIE. Oh. Can you?

PHILIP. No, actually, he can't. He doesn't work here.

DENNIS. She needs somebody to look at it, Philip. What's the big deal?

PHILIP. The "big deal" maybe would be the fact that you are utterly unqualified.

DENNIS. Then why don't you look at it? You're not doing anything.

PHILIP. In fact I am doing something.

DENNIS. What?

PHILIP. I don't have to justify my actions to you.

DENNIS. "Justify your actions," stop being such an asshole and look at her stamps!

PHILIP. Listen. I tolerate you. I *tolerate* you. But if you think that means you have rights here –

JACKIE. It's okay, I can –

DENNIS. He's not doing anything, he'll look at it. Just look at it!

PHILIP. Fine!

(*beat*)

I'll look at it.

(*He gestures to her. Perplexed, she takes the album to the desk and sets it down. She waits. He continues to read his book. He turns a page. She watches him, more and more anxious and annoyed.*)

JACKIE. Are you going to...

PHILIP. I said I would look at it. You need to leave it.

JACKIE. You want me to –

PHILIP. My fee is two percent of the net worth, or two thousand dollars.

JACKIE. You want two thousand dollars just to look at it?

PHILIP. I am looking at it now. Looking is for free. Using thirty-seven years of experience and expertise to evaluate the specific worth of your property costs two thousand dollars.

JACKIE. I didn't, I didn't, um – I don't have two thousand dollars.

PHILIP. Well, that's a problem then, isn't it?

(**DENNIS** *stands, goes to the counter.*)

DENNIS. Philip, you know, you can be a real jerk. I will look at it.

PHILIP. That would be very useful to her if you actually knew anything.

DENNIS. I know plenty.

JACKIE. I just need to know, to, I just, because if it is worth something, then if I sold it –

DENNIS. Totally, I get it. People do this all the time. He's supposed to do it, but he's a little, don't worry about him. I'll look at it for you.

(*He starts to page through it.*)

PHILIP. This is not in any way a professional evaluation.

DENNIS. Relax, would you? You're not going to help her, what's the big deal?

JACKIE. How much, uh –

DENNIS. Nothing. This is free.

JACKIE. Great.

PHILIP. I cannot vouch for this man. He knows next to nothing.

DENNIS. Wow, look at this. Where'd you get this?

JACKIE. My mom had it. It's been in our family.

DENNIS. She's got an inverted Jenny, Phil. It's a little bit of a mess, the colors are compromised, unfortunately, by what looks like water damage, see this line here? That's not good. But it's a significant stamp.

JACKIE. Is it worth anything, even with the...

DENNIS. Hard to say. Maybe three thousand?

JACKIE. Dollars? Three thousand –

PHILIP. (*sneering*) An inverted Jenny. There are so many forgeries floating around out there people are starting to use them to mail in their absentee ballots. Besides which how would you know the difference? Tell me what the difference is. You can't because you don't know.

DENNIS. She's got some nice stuff here, Phil. Couple of Zepplins. These are nice stamps.

JACKIE. Three thousand dollars? For one stamp?

DENNIS. What's your name?

JACKIE. Jackie.

DENNIS. You have some lovely stamps here, Jackie. This is a nice collection.

JACKIE. It belonged to a relative. He's dead now.

DENNIS. Well, this is a beautiful collection, he was an artist.

PHILIP. (*aghast at this bullshit*) Oh my god.

DENNIS. What do you care, Philip? She asked, I'm telling her. It's a shame to sell this, Jackie, I hope you have a good reason.

JACKIE. Well, I, you know, yes I do. I have a really good reason.

DENNIS. You want to sell the whole thing together or break it up?

JACKIE. Which is worth more?

DENNIS. Well, it depends on different, you know, different...

(*He stops paging, stares at one of the pages.*)

JACKIE. Whichever you think is better.

PHILIP. He is not qualified to give you anything resembling a legitimate estimate. This man is not a philatelist. He is not an employee of this store, this store does not endorse anything he has to say. I barely know him. He is an acquaintance, at best.

DENNIS. (*looking at* **JACKIE**) Where did you get this?

JACKIE. I told you my... what?

(*She watches him, alert now. He is staring at a page.*)

JACKIE. (*continuing*) What? Is it worth something?

PHILIP. (*annoyed*) This is ludicrous. Let me, let me, he doesn't –

(**PHILIP** *reaches over to take the book.* **DENNIS** *slams the book shut before he can.*)

DENNIS. (*friendly*) This is a nice collection. You got a few nice things, it's okay.

JACKIE. Yeah but is it...

DENNIS. No, it's nice, it's a nice collection. Like he said I'm not really an expert. That one stamp, it's a good stamp, the inverted Jenny is rare and a lot of people are looking for them? But yours isn't really in terrific shape. Besides, unfortunately he is right about those forgeries. There were a whole mess of forgeries that hit the market in the eighties, that's more than likely what your stamp is.

PHILIP. As if you know anything about forgeries.

DENNIS. You were right. There's not a lot here, for you, Phil. For her, this is I'm sure a treasure. Your relative had a lovely collection. But in his terms, it's not worth anything. You should take it home.

JACKIE. He said, but he said you don't know anything.

DENNIS. I know a lot.

JACKIE. He said –

DENNIS. (*gentle*) Go home.

(*He gives her her book. Blackout.*)

Scene 2

(**DENNIS** *and* **STERLING**, *in a coffee shop.*)

STERLING. I don't believe you.

DENNIS. I saw it.

STERLING. You saw it.

DENNIS. Yes. I touched it.

STERLING. You touched it.

DENNIS. (*firm*) Yes I did.

STERLING. I don't believe you.

DENNIS. I don't care if you believe me or not. I half don't believe it myself.

(*They think for a moment.*)

STERLING. It's a fake.

DENNIS. It's not a fake.

STERLING. You only saw it for a second.

DENNIS. He was right over my shoulder! What was I supposed to do?

STERLING. Shit. Fuck. I don't believe you.

DENNIS. Fuck you.

(*Beat.*)

STERLING. So this person just walked in, opened a book, and showed it to you.

DENNIS. Yes!

STERLING. What kind of shape was it in?

DENNIS. Uncanceled, It's mounted on one of those old Dennison things, the really good ones that peel right off? There might be the barest memory of an older mount along one of the borders but other than the sliver of a suggestion of that previous mount, I would have to say it is ... pristine.

STERLING. Fuck, that's...

DENNIS. I saw it!

STERLING. And then she went home?

DENNIS. She did.

STERLING. She walked in, and walked out, you let her just walk out with it?

DENNIS. Well, I followed her.

STERLING. Where'd she go?

DENNIS. She went home.

STERLING. Where?

DENNIS. Oh no no. No no no.

STERLING. This story is shit. You think I don't know when I'm being played?

DENNIS. I think you do know when you're being played, Sterling, which is why you're still sitting here.

STERLING. Fuck you, you little piece of shit. You bring me this fucking preposterous story about some girl with a – fuck you. *Fuck you.* Life is short my friend, and it's getting shorter, you bring stories like this to the table. You ask yourself, what do you want out of life? I advise you. At moments like this, you are stepping out over the abyss, for what? How much money is it worth to you, Dennis, to risk what will befall you, I don't say possibly, I say certainly, what will befall a person like you, stepping onto the highwire of complete bullshit that just came out of your mouth.

DENNIS. How much do I want? Is that what you just asked me? How much money do I expect you to pay me to make this happen?

(*beat, happy*)

A lot, Sterling. Really, quite a lot.

(*Beat.*)

STERLING. You're lying, or she is.

DENNIS. I'm not lying. And she doesn't know how to lie.

STERLING. Since you spent so much time with her. And you know her so well.

DENNIS. She reads comic books, Sterling. This girl is a lamb.

(*A beat, while* **STERLING** *considers.*)

STERLING. I don't believe you. I'm leaving.

(*He stands to go.* **DENNIS** *leans back in his chair, lets him get all the way across the room, then calls after him.*)

DENNIS. I didn't tell you everything.

(**STERLING** *stops, but doesn't turn.*)

DENNIS. (*continuing*) There are two of them. The One Penny *and* the Two Penny.

STERLING. Oh you motherfucker.

(**STERLING** *turns and looks at* **DENNIS.** **DENNIS** *shrugs, laughs. He is very happy. Blackout.*)

Scene 3

(**MARY**, *at home. She is surrounded by boxes.*)

MARY. Mauritius is a paradise tropical island in the Indian Ocean, off the coast of Africa, east of Madagascar.

JACKIE. I don't need to know about the island. I was curious about the stamps.

(*She enters, carrying a box full of stuff, drops it on the floor.*)

MARY. But you have to know all of it, that's what's so fun! Mauritius, what do I remember? Volcanic in origin, surrounded by coral reefs, what else? The Labourdonannais orchards –

JACKIE. These are all the bills. Most of them I can't even read, to tell the truth. You look at it, there's so many numbers, I have no idea what we owe. Every time I try to figure it out my head starts to hurt. I feel so stupid.

MARY. (*off a box*) Oh, look, her jewelry! Did you bring this down?

JACKIE. Yes, I, yes, I did.

MARY. Let's see what else do I know about Mauritius. They have beautiful beaches. I dislike the beach, don't you? All that sand. Do you like the beach?

JACKIE. I've never been.

MARY. You've never been?

JACKIE. No, I've never been.

MARY. To the beach? Any beach?

JACKIE. No. I've never been to any beach.

MARY. You've never seen the ocean.

JACKIE. Oh god. You know –

MARY. I just find that –

JACKIE. I'm not –

MARY. What? Why can't I even comment?

JACKIE. Because there's nothing to comment on. I've just never seen it. I will see the ocean. I will, I'll see it, I'll see it some day. I'm young. I'm I'm *young.*

MARY. (*smiling at her, lovely*) Of course you are! Of course
you are. We don't have to talk about it. Let's see, where
were we?

JACKIE. The stamps?

MARY. Oh yes. They had this stamp, the Mauritians – Mauritians, that sounds like Martians, could that be right?
Oh well, actually, it wouldn't have been the Mauritians,
it would have been the British, they took it over back
when they were you know, taking things over, and in
1847, they printed one of the first postage stamps on
earth. The fifth country, I think. The head of the young
Queen Victoria – oh, look at this! I remember this!

(*She holds up an ugly broach.*)

JACKIE. Take it. Take all of it.

MARY. I'm sure you want some of it.

JACKIE. It's not worth anything.

MARY. Maybe not to anyone else, but to us – oh, look at this!

JACKIE. (*off the stamp book*) So it's worth a lot of money then.
This Mauritian stamp.

MARY. Both of them. The One Penny and the Two Penny
Post Office. Together. They're considered the crown
jewel of philately. It's quite a spectacular error.

JACKIE. Error?

MARY. Well, that's what makes it so valuable, the errors are
what make it – well, you don't know anything about
stamps, do you?

JACKIE. So what's the "error?"

MARY. Alongside her face are the words "Post Office." The
printer was supposed to print the words "Post Paid."
Post *paid*. Of course once you know that it makes sense,
why would you put "Post Office" on a stamp? I wonder
that sometimes. What was going through that man's
head. While he made the first postage stamp, and put
the wrong words on it, out there in the middle of the
Indian Ocean.

(*She thinks about this, moved.* JACKIE *thinks too, looking at the stamps.*)

JACKIE. So how much, a thousand, a hundred thousand? How much are stamps worth?

MARY. I have no idea how much it's worth, it's beside the point. I couldn't possibly sell it. Oh! Oh. I'm sorry. But you do realize that those are my stamps. Don't you? He was my grandfather. He wasn't your grandfather. Those are – my stamps.

JACKIE. Mom said, she gave the stamps to me, because she didn't know for sure but she said they might be worth something –

MARY. Well, but – these weren't *her* stamps.

JACKIE. She gave them to me.

MARY. If you want the jewelry –

JACKIE. I don't want the jewelry. I already said I don't want the jewelry.

MARY. But they were my grandfather's stamps, they're not part of the general, this isn't –

JACKIE. This isn't what? I mean, you weren't here –

MARY. That's not exactly –

JACKIE. Not exactly what, not exactly true? That you weren't here?

MARY. Not exactly relevant, I was going to say.

JACKIE. It was relevant to me. That's why I asked, so many times. You got my messages, right? We really needed you, I needed, you know –

MARY. Yes, yes yes but – I'm sorry but could we stay on the point please?

JACKIE. The point is when Mom was — even when she was so sick, she she she gave the stamps to me and you weren't here –

MARY. Look, I don't want to, we're just having a conversation. You asked about the stamps.

JACKIE. Yes I did, that's right I did –

MARY. So we're having a conversation! There's no will and it would be terrible if we had to probate anything, that would take years, and involve all sorts of legal issues, so it's great that we can talk about what is yours, and what

is mine. I'm really thrilled to have the stamps back. I
I don't know how they ended up in mother's hands.
Grandfather and I spent so much time with these
stamps. Making catalogues, and lists. Correspond-
ing with other dealers. Grandfather once, obviously
this is long before I was born, but he actually had an
extended correspondence with FDR about the Two
Penny Post Office, he wanted to buy it but grandfather
would never let it go. You just wouldn't. Let it go. You
wouldn't.

(*Beat.*)

JACKIE. Wow. An extended correspondence with FDR.
That's incredible. How much did he offer?

MARY. I don't know that they ever got that far.

JACKIE. (*beat*) Maybe you could look through these boxes,
I cleared out that closet upstairs. It doesn't look like
anything to me but what do I know.

(*There is a buzz at the door.* **MARY** *continues to page
through the book of stamps while* **JACKIE** *continues to
work.*)

MARY. Look, the inverted Jenny! This was one of my favor-
ites. I used to pretend that grandfather and I were
flying in the airplane, upside down!

JACKIE. Are you getting the door?

MARY. What?

JACKIE. The door, didn't you hear the door?

MARY. Oh, I thought you were getting it.

JACKIE. I'm working.

MARY. All you have to do is ask.

JACKIE. That's what I'm doing, I'm asking.

MARY. And I'm getting it!

(*She smiles and goes to answer the door. After she is
gone,* **JACKIE** *is alone in the room for a moment.*)

JACKIE. (*to herself*) I hate her. I hate her so much. Oh god,
I hate her.

(*She looks around, goes to the chair where* **MARY** *left the stamps, picks up the stamp book and moves it to her side of the room. Then she goes back to work.* **MARY** *reenters, with* **DENNIS**.)

MARY. Your friend is here!

JACKIE. (*without looking up*) I don't have any friends.

DENNIS. It's Dennis. Hey, Jackie.

(*She looks up. He smiles at her, reaches out to shake hands. She takes his hand and at the last minute he draws her in, kisses her on the cheek.*)

DENNIS. (*continuing*) Good to see you.

JACKIE. What are *you* doing here?

DENNIS. We met the other day, when you came over to Phil's.

JACKIE. I remember. What are you doing here?

DENNIS. (*to* **MARY**) Hi, I'm Dennis. What's your name?

MARY. I'm Mary, I'm Jackie's sister. Her half-sister. Her much older half sister, I'm afraid.

DENNIS. Yeah, yeah, Jackie mentioned you.

MARY. Oh, I'm sure.

DENNIS. (*a quick glance to* **JACKIE**, *sizing this up*) No, she did. She said you were the pretty one.

MARY. (*laughing at this nonsense*) So how do you two know each other?

DENNIS. We met, actually, at my friend Phil's store, just yesterday. She came in with this –

JACKIE. (*overlap, cool*) Mary, you know, listen, maybe Dennis would like some iced tea. Dennis, would you like some iced tea? Or lemonade, or water, maybe some cookies?

(**DENNIS** *looks at her. Beat.*)

DENNIS. Sure, that'd be great.

JACKIE. Mary? Could you bring Dennis some refreshments?

MARY. Of course. Iced tea? Maybe a beer?

DENNIS. A beer would be great, Mary. Thanks.

(MARY *nods and goes, leaving* JACKIE *and* DENNIS *alone.*)

DENNIS. (*continuing*) I know, it's kind of a little bold for me to just show up like this. I'm sorry. But I really needed to talk to you.

JACKIE. How did you know where I live?

DENNIS. Yeah, well, after you left Phil's the other day, I followed you home. Listen, do you mind if I...

(*He points and instinctively moves to the table, where the book of stamps sits, still open to the page with the One Penny and Two Penny Post Office stamps.* JACKIE *crosses swiftly and takes the book. He looks at her.*)

DENNIS. (*continuing*) Sorry. There's just a couple of stamps in there, that I thought were kind of interesting.

JACKIE. The One Penny and the Two Penny Post Office.

DENNIS. (*beat*) Yeah.

JACKIE. They're from Mauritius.

DENNIS. (*recovering swiftly*) Yes, that's uh, that's right.

JACKIE. It's in the Indian Ocean. Off the coast of Africa. East of Madagascar. It was only the fifth country in the world to issue postage stamps. The post office stamps are considered the crown jewel of philately.

DENNIS. Wow. That's pretty good. You know a lot. Because you didn't. Yesterday. Know much, I mean. Well. You're an interesting girl.

(*He sits.*)

JACKIE. Look. You can't stay here. If you want to talk about those stamps –

DENNIS. I do want to talk about them. Are you selling them?

JACKIE. Leave me your number and I'll call you.

DENNIS. Do you know how much they're worth?

JACKIE. I said, I'll call you.

DENNIS. She doesn't know, does she? That you're selling the stamps.

JACKIE. She doesn't need to know.

DENNIS. Is she the one I should be talking to?

JACKIE. They're not her stamps.

DENNIS. Does she know that?

JACKIE. Look. You talk to her, it's not going to get you anywhere.

DENNIS. Maybe I should find that out for myself.

JACKIE. You do, and you take yourself out of the running.

DENNIS. "The running?"

JACKIE. That's right.

DENNIS. Well, that's a very interesting thing to say, from a girl who is increasingly interesting. You have other offers?

JACKIE. Yes, I have other offers.

DENNIS. Really?

JACKIE. Yes. I contacted another dealer and I have a lot of interest. So if you're interested in buying them you need to speak up now, because...

DENNIS. Oh, buy them.

JACKIE. Yes buy them. Of course buy them.

DENNIS. It's not of course, of course is the last thing this is.

(*Beat.*)

JACKIE. Look, if you don't want to buy them –

DENNIS. I didn't say that either.

JACKIE. So make me an offer.

DENNIS. Oh, shit no.

JACKIE. Okay, thank you so much for stopping by.

(*She stands, to show him out. He stands, and blocks her.*)

DENNIS. You make me an offer.

JACKIE. You want me to make you an offer?

DENNIS. Is that a problem?

JACKIE. I own them! I don't have to offer you anything!

DENNIS. Tell me what you want for them.

JACKIE. Why don't you just tell me what you're willing to pay, and I'll tell you if that's enough.

DENNIS. Why don't you tell me what you think they're worth, and I'll tell you if I'll pay that.

JACKIE. Look. I know you think I don't know anything?

DENNIS. Yeah, I actually, I do think that. For a minute there I thought you maybe knew a few things, but I don't think that anymore.

JACKIE. I already got an offer on these stamps. I know what they're worth.

DENNIS. Then why don't you tell me what it is.

    (*beat*)

You grow less interesting every second.

JACKIE. Oh yeah? Because it seems to me, as long as I'm holding the stamps and you're not, I'm still pretty fucking interesting.

MARY. (*reentering*) Here we are! Oh, you're not leaving are you?

JACKIE. Yes, sadly he has to go.

DENNIS. Actually I can stay. You know, that thing I had to do, I don't really have to do it. I'd love to stay. Thanks, Mary.

    (*He takes his beer from her, and sits.*)

JACKIE. Well, I'm actually, I have a lot to do, I'm working right now, so this isn't a great time for me. For a visit.

DENNIS. You go ahead. Mary and I can hang out.

MARY. Oh!

DENNIS. Jackie was telling me about the stamp collection.

MARY. Really?

DENNIS. Does that surprise you?

JACKIE. Listen.

MARY. Well, she was just – she doesn't –

DENNIS. Know anything about it.

MARY. (*laughing*) Well –

JACKIE. Hey. Dennis.

DENNIS. It's okay. I could tell. You're the stamp collector, I'm betting.

MARY. My grandfather.

DENNIS. What was he like?

MARY. He was wonderful, he really was. My father died when I was quite young, so he was the only father I knew.

DENNIS. Your father's father.

MARY. Yes.

JACKIE. Mary, maybe this isn't the best time.

DENNIS. And maybe it is. You don't want to talk about it. But maybe Mary would like to talk about it. It seems like she and her grandfather were close.

MARY. Oh, he was everything to me.

DENNIS. You should talk about it. You too, Jackie.

JACKIE. Would you stop using my name, Dennis? I find it increasingly unnerving having you talk to me like this, Dennis; I really do.

DENNIS. Is she always like this, Mary?

MARY. Well...

DENNIS. Oh, you poor thing.

JACKIE. Yes, that's hilarious, Dennis –

DENNIS. Oh, chill out, would you? I'm trying to be nice here. I mean, I can see you've both been through something, I'm just trying to – I don't know –

MARY. She didn't tell you?

DENNIS. She won't tell me anything, Mary.

JACKIE. It's very personal, Mary, and I don't think, I really prefer –

MARY. Our mother. Passed.

DENNIS. Oh.

MARY. It was very sudden.

JACKIE. Okay, that is not strictly true, Mary, she was sick for a long – . Hm. You know, Dennis, I'm sure you understand that it's just not a good time, today –

DENNIS. It seems like it's a good time for Mary.

JACKIE. But it's a terrifically terrible time, for me.

MARY. (*under her breath*) It's always a terrible time for you.

JACKIE. We are not talking about this, Mary!

MARY. Why not? Why not?

JACKIE. (*snapping*) Because I don't want to!

MARY. Why? Why is it so hard for you to understand, I didn't have the time you had, to to to get used to what was happening –

JACKIE. (*overlap*) Stop acting, it's your own fault! She asked you to come, she begged you, and you stayed away. That was your choice.

MARY. It had been so long since anyone was interested, years, what was I supposed to do? Oh now she's dying, she wants to see you now. I had feelings about that. I don't apologize for that. What, she only wants to see me when she's dying?

JACKIE. She was dying! She wanted to see you!

MARY. Well I needed a little time to work that through, all right?

JACKIE. Yes, that's a terrific point, except there wasn't any time! She was dying!

MARY. I'm sorry. I didn't mean to get into this. You've been so kind to me, Dennis. I really appreciate it. It's been hard, going through what we're going through. I'm sure that's what you sense with Jackie.

DENNIS. Absolutely.

(*beat*)

Do you want a glass of wine or something?

MARY. I'm fine. I'm fine. I shouldn't have just erupted like that, I'm so sorry.

DENNIS. Please don't apologize. The death of a parent, that's huge.

JACKIE. You know it really is and I really really think that Mary and I need a little privacy right now, Dennis. Please.

DENNIS. How did she die?

MARY. Cancer.

JACKIE. Oh my God.

DENNIS. (*to* **MARY**) And you lost your father as well?

MARY. Oh well, that was years ago.

DENNIS. That's rough, Mary. I mean, that's just tough.

MARY. Thank you.

DENNIS. (*putting it together*) And so Jackie's your half sister, but you have the same mother – well, had, I'm so sorry – so, that means Jackie's father – where'd he go?

JACKIE. (*a real eruption*) Mind your own fucking business! That is none of your – you know, you need to get out of here. Just GET OUT OF HERE.

DENNIS. Whoa. Jackie. I am so sorry. Did I step into a sensitive subject?

(*There is a pause.* **JACKIE** *takes a breath. She reaches over and takes the beer from* **MARY**, *drinks.*)

JACKIE. It is a bit of a sensitive subject, Dennis. I really apologize. To you too, Mary. I'm clearly just not myself these days. You know, Dennis, I am so glad you stopped by and I think you and I have a lot to talk over and I'm hoping we can do that.

DENNIS. Oh, good.

JACKIE. Yeah. I'm more than willing, I really want to hear you out, and talk things over and things like that. But right now, really, really – it's such not the right time.

DENNIS. I totally understand. Look. Let's talk about something else. What can we talk about? The stamps. Why don't you tell me about them, Mary?

(*He hands her the album. She touches it, reverential.*)

DENNIS. (*continuing*) You know, Franklin Roosevelt collected stamps.

MARY. (*laughing a little*) Of course I knew that. My grandfather actually corresponded with FDR. He wanted to buy one of our stamps!

DENNIS. Did he?

MARY. My grandfather had both a One Penny AND a Two Penny Post Office. From Mauritius. They're very very rare.

DENNIS. The crown jewel of philately.

MARY. You know stamps?

DENNIS. A little.

(**DENNIS** *smiles at her, friendly, while* **JACKIE** *watches this, appalled. Blackout.*)

Scene 4

(**PHILIP**'s *shop. He is at the counter, reading again.*
STERLING *stands in the doorway.*)

STERLING. Hey.

PHILIP. (*glancing up*) Yes?

STERLING. How you doing?

PHILIP. Oh.

STERLING. Yeah, hi.

PHILIP. He's not here.

STERLING. No, I know. I mean, I see that.

PHILIP. Well.

STERLING. You talk to him today?

PHILIP. No.

STERLING. Yesterday?

PHILIP. (*a sigh*) Yes. He was here yesterday.

STERLING. Yeah? How was that?

PHILIP. How was it?

STERLING. Yeah, you know, anything going on?

PHILIP. Not that I know of.

STERLING. Yeah?

PHILIP. Do you want something, Sterling? Do you want to look at something, or...

(*He thinks for a minute, then remembers.*)

STERLING. Or what?

PHILIP. Nothing.

(*beat*)

Did he ... tell you something?

STERLING. Is there something to tell?

PHILIP. No. There isn't. He just sat here. That's all that happened, that's all that ever happens. If anything shows up, my understanding is he'll tell you, but nothing ever does. Okay? Nothing ever does.

STERLING. That's not what he says.

(*There is a beat.* **PHILIP** *thinks about this, then shrugs, laughs a little.*)

PHILIP. You want to look through my case? I'd be happy to have you look through this stuff. I don't know why you'd want to, I'm pretty sure this isn't going to mean anything to you, and I don't know why you think, whatever it is you do think –

STERLING. I don't think anything.

PHILIP. Okay. Okay then, let me show you what I got, maybe you'll get lucky and I'll get lucky and retire on the vast sums of money you'll shower on my unworthy head.

STERLING. I don't need to do that.

PHILIP. (*beat*) What do you want? Sterling? Just tell me what you want, okay?

STERLING. I want to hear about the girl.

PHILIP. What girl?

STERLING. You really want to play it like that, Phil?

PHILIP. Oh my god. Does this actually get you things, talking like this?

STERLING. Yeah, actually it does.

PHILIP. Well good because frankly it seems kind of silly to me.

STERLING. That's fine. That's fine, Phil. Now why don't you tell me about the girl.

PHILIP. Was there a girl who came in here yesterday, that Dennis talked to who had some stamps, is this the question you're asking me? Yes. The answer is yes, there was a girl who came in who had some stamps and Dennis talked to her. Now can I ask you something? Did Dennis tell you this, that he saw a girl in here and she showed him some stamps?

STERLING. Yes he did.

PHILIP. Then why are you asking me about it?

STERLING. I'm asking about it because I'm trying to be polite.

PHILIP. Hey, don't strain yourself.

STERLING. Philip, I don't. I just offer you an opportunity. I know you've got a problem, you think I took something from you at some point, you can't get over something that happened so long ago no one gives a shit, I realize that. I'm coming in here and I'm being nice out of sensitivity to something I really, a rat's ass would be a step up, in my book, to what you're holding onto. We both know that. And it is an irritant to a person, let's say a person was stupid, at one time in the past, and I'm not talking about myself, but someone behaves in a stupid way, no one has to say anything about that except that that person needs to own his own stupidity and not wallow in some sense of blame or victimhood, you're so interested in victimhood? Go watch T.V., that is not a world that interests me. It's an irritant. So there is some question, in my mind? How long this attempt at civility is going to survive here. Under these circumstances. Because due respect, I'm better in a situation when I can just be direct.

(*beat*)

This is an olive branch, Philip.

PHILIP. Well, you know, I'm touched. I mean, that's terrific. All of this, what you just said, I feel a lot better, I mean you were right, you're right, I have been holding onto that silly little matter, how long ago was that –

STERLING. Eight –

PHILIP. Eight years! Is that how long? Wow, time flies doesn't it?

STERLING. You ever hear from her?

PHILIP. That's not – I am not –

STERLING. I'm asking as a friend.

PHILIP. I am not talking about her!

STERLING. Eight years, due respect, is a long enough time to contemplate that maybe there was a problem in the marriage.

PHILIP. (*overlap*) I am not talking about her!

STERLING. Just a casual observation. A casual, friendly –

PHILIP. What do you want, Sterling? You want to look at my stamps, is that what you want? Then look at them! No? Then shut the fuck up and get out of my shop. I mean it. I don't care about your money. I don't want you here. I don't... I...

(*Exasperated,* **PHILIP** *starts to put his stamps away. Then he stops, looks at them, sad.*)

PHILIP. Whatever. I have some nice... you know, there's a really lovely set of Columbians, someone brought them in, I, they're canceled but the color is quite good, quite...

(*Beat.* **PHILIP** *stops, sighs, looks at him, bracing himself.*)

PHILIP. (*continuing*) Okay. What was in there?

STERLING. I was hoping you could tell me.

PHILIP. I didn't see it!

STERLING. I don't believe you.

PHILIP. What would I – what would I gain? If Dennis has told you about it already, what would I gain, by lying?

STERLING. I'm not saying you're lying.

PHILIP. I didn't see it. I didn't look.

STERLING. You didn't even look.

PHILIP. No, I didn't. How many times do we have to do this –

STERLING. HEY. ASSHOLE.

(*beat*)

Don't misunderstand me.

PHILIP. I didn't look, Sterling! I don't know what was in there. Whatever Dennis told you, if you think he's lying, or trying to pull something, I can't help you because I didn't look. I'm sick of looking. Every day there's one more pathetic, look at my stamps. What are they worth. My great uncle told my third cousin that this stamp was so valuable, it's worth a fortune, buy my stamp, save my pathetic life, it's a miracle! A miracle that I just pulled out of a back drawer! They don't even look at ... they don't even see them. Fuck it. I didn't look.

(*beat*)

So whatever he told you, I can't tell you.

STERLING. He said it was a post office.

PHILIP. (*a short laugh*) Well, then he is a liar.

STERLING. You said you didn't see it.

PHILIP. If he told you she has a post office –

STERLING. He told me she has two.

PHILIP. That's insane. He's lying.

(*a beat*)

He's lying. They aren't out there. They're like a myth. Two post office stamps? Just lying around some old man's stamp collection? Maybe he's got an undiscovered Shakespeare sonnet in there, too. And you're actually checking this story out? C'mere, I have a bridge.

STERLING. Hey. Do I look amused? Because let me tell you something which has in fact occurred to me. If there's anyone in this situation who has the talent and the know how to pull off anything resembling a scam, it would be you, Phil. Dennis has the nerve, but you're the one would know how to do it. So when Dennis calls me and says 'meet me at Phil's, we have to talk about this stamp,' I'm wondering why that is. What you have to do with any of it. And I'm interested in hearing your explanation on that.

PHILIP. What?

STERLING. God, I don't want to have to hit you.

PHILIP. I don't want that either. What are you asking me? Am I cheating you? I'm just standing here. I just, I know nothing about anything you are talking about. As far as I'm concerned, you are completely out of your fucking mind –

(**STERLING** *picks up* **PHILIP** *and swings him out from behind the counter, about to hurl him at the wall.*)

PHILIP. (*continuing*) Wait wait, no wait – Sterling – wait – I didn't mean it, I meant all I mean was why would, I'm the one telling you that Dennis is lying, how would I be in on that? Sterling – listen to me, please don't hurt me, please I would never ever PLEASE –

(*The door opens;* **DENNIS** *enters.*)

DENNIS. (*overlap*) Whoa whoa whoa, hey Sterling chill out! What is with you, let him go, we need him, could you not hurt him? WE NEED HIM.

(*He pulls* **STERLING** *off of* **PHILIP**, *who backs away quickly and goes behind the counter.*)

PHILIP. I'm calling the cops on both of you.

STERLING. Yeah, go ahead and do it then! Do it!

DENNIS. Would you two relax? Really, Sterling, for heaven's sake, where are your manners? I'm sorry, Phil, I really am. He's just a little excited.

PHILIP. I don't want anything to do with this.

DENNIS. You haven't heard what this is yet.

PHILIP. You told him some fairy tale about a post office –

DENNIS. Not "a" post office, two of them, the One Penny *and* the Two Penny.

PHILIP. It's a crock.

DENNIS. It's not. I just went by and saw them again. They're very very real, and they're in surprisingly good shape. They were originally purchased from a dealer in Lucerne in 1938, 1939, somewhere around there. I even got the name of the dealer. We tried to call but not surprisingly he's not in business anymore, although just for fun, we did check up on the provenance of several of the other stamps, and they hold up! That old guy knew what he was doing! Those stamps are real!

PHILIP. Thirty nine in Lucerne? They were probably stolen from some poor dead Jew.

DENNIS. Did you just hear what I said? They're real!

PHILIP. I will tell you if they're real or not.

DENNIS. That's what I was thinking.

PHILIP. Oh no. No. I'm not helping you. Forget it.

DENNIS. Philip, this is a free offer. Out of respect. I mean, I found them in your shop.

PHILIP. You didn't find them! She walked in!

DENNIS. Yeah, she did, and you wouldn't wouldn't even look at them. You're lucky I'm even talking to you. I didn't have to cut you in.

PHILIP. Cut me into what? You don't have anything!

DENNIS. Neither do you. What do you got here, a couple of Columbians and the rest is shit, Phil. You're off the map, in every way. Don't you even want to see them? I've touched them. Don't you want to do that?

STERLING. Fuck him; we don't need him. Let's go.

DENNIS. This is your chance, Phil; you're about to lose it.

STERLING. He's a has-been for a reason, Dennis!

DENNIS. He knows what he's doing!

STERLING. Yeah that's why he let her walk in and out without even looking at what she had. We don't need him. Let's go get my fucking stamps.

(*He heads for the door.*)

DENNIS. You're going to take my word on it, then? That they're real?

STERLING. I know people.

DENNIS. (*mad now*) I know you do! So do I. And we can take this girl, and her stamps to any of them; we can go see Julian or Stuart or Paulie; we can fly to London and have Richard fucking Dempsey himself validate those stamps and any one of those people will tell that girl what those stamps are really worth.

PHILIP. What makes you think I won't?

DENNIS. Intuition. So maybe we don't need him, Sterling. But we sure as hell could fucking use him.

PHILIP. So you actually expect me to help you rob that girl.

DENNIS. We'll pay her! I never said we wouldn't pay her!

PHILIP. Not what they're worth.

DENNIS. You don't know what they're worth; you haven't seen them yet! Come on Phil this is a gift, the skies opened yesterday, and the heavens shone their light upon us and that girl walked in here with a One Penny and a TWO PENNY POST OFFICE, and it was a gift, a gift to me and a gift to you and a gift to our good friend Sterling here. This is happening! And it can be easy, or it can be hard. I vote for easy.

(*Beat.*)

PHILIP. For a fee. I'll do it for a fee.

DENNIS. A very good fee. She's bringing them over tonight.

STERLING. You just left them there?

DENNIS. She's not going anywhere!

STERLING. What's she asking for them?

DENNIS. We didn't quite get that far.

STERLING. And she has no idea what they're worth.

DENNIS. No.

(*beat*)

No.

STERLING. You don't think.

DENNIS. When she sees a suitcase full of cash, she's not going to ask a lot of questions about what she might get for them if she spent months on line trying to nurse a better offer out of some shithead in Tokyo. Don't worry about it. You'll get a good price.

STERLING. She goes on line we're fucked.

DENNIS. I can handle the internet, please!

STERLING. You seem pretty sure of yourself. Call me crazy but I do have to ask, why is that?

DENNIS. Would you relax? I'm telling you, there's damage there! Damage. This is a desperate person, Sterling; she'll do what we want.

STERLING. What's she doing carrying them around anyway? Why aren't they in a deposit box somewhere?

DENNIS. What do you care?

PHILIP. He thinks you've cooked up some big plan to con him.

DENNIS. He's high strung.

STERLING. This isn't a joke. I can feel them now. The stamps. You know this about me. When I want something? It happens.

DENNIS. I know that Sterling, that's why –

STERLING. (*overlapping*) You touched them. I can't stand that, that you touched them. You think I don't know what that means? Fuck you. The first time I touched a Columbian, I will never forget it. An 1893 four dollar, beautiful, a rosy pink, the perforations, pure, the head of Isabella and Columbus facing each other across time. This thing was gorgeous, I'm telling you, your Columbians are shit, Phil, this stamp was beyond reason, the perfection, everybody knows to look for the mistakes, that's a given and I love that too, the errors? But the perfection, people don't talk about. I got a Hindenberg crash cover, I paid sixty thousand dollars for it; I know its worth, historically, and I respect it, but am I moved? A One Penny and a Two Penny Post Office. And they're good, huh? I saw them once, the Royal Philatelic Society had a fucking show, fuck them, the self-righteous bastards, putting a fucking piece of glass in front of those stamps. Their collection was shit anyway. It wasn't shit but it wasn't good. And they're good huh? You're telling me they're good?

DENNIS. Pristine.

STERLING. Fuck you. This deal doesn't make, you are fucked, my friend.

DENNIS. Relax, would you? It's going to make! Everyone wants this deal to make.

STERLING. Including her.

DENNIS. Especially her! Sterling! I would not mess with you on things like this. I know what you're feeling. I respect it utterly. Now. I always say cash makes a big impression, and that's what's gonna close this. How liquid are you these days? Can you put your hands on a suitcase full of cash?

STERLING. What do you think?

DENNIS. I think I have a motivated buyer on my hands. Phil, don't go anywhere. We'll be back.

(*They go.* **PHILIP** *sits for a moment, then stands, pulls out a phone from behind the desk. He dials.*)

PHILIP. (*on phone*) Hey, it's Phil. Listen, this girl came here yesterday, said she bought some comic books from you, and asked about selling some stamps. Yeah, she did, and you know, she left them here, and I forgot to get her address, or her phone – oh, you do. Yeah, could I have that?

(*He listens. Blackout.*)

Scene 5

(**JACKIE** *sits alone, in the dark. She holds the stamp book, clutching it to her chest.* **MARY** *enters.*)

MARY. Oh! It's so dark, I didn't know you were in here. What are you doing in the dark?

JACKIE. Thinking.

MARY. Thinking. That sounds so mysterious. What are you thinking about?

JACKIE. Our situation here.

(**MARY** *turns on the lights.*)

MARY. "Our situation?" I wasn't aware that we had a situation.

(**JACKIE** *sets the stamp book down, near her.*)

JACKIE. I was thinking... I was thinking about how, I know you weren't here. And, I know you're upset about that.

MARY. I'm not upset.

JACKIE. This afternoon, you said –

MARY. I'm a little upset, of course I am.

JACKIE. Yes. Yes! Because, you know, that's what I've been thinking about. I've been thinking, that I should tell you what happened. All of it. I never told anybody. But I'll tell you. And then, we'll be in it, together. And then you can understand. Maybe that's why you're so angry.

MARY. I'm not angry.

JACKIE. You're kind of angry. This afternoon –

MARY. Well of course I'm a little angry. I feel very, of course I feel torn, my mother is dead and I didn't really know her or you.

JACKIE. I do want you to know me. That's what I'm saying. If you want, to to know. I'll tell you.

MARY. Jackie, I want to know anything you want to tell me.

JACKIE. Good.

MARY. Yes. Good.

JACKIE. Because a lot happened. After you left. It wasn't just when she died. That wasn't the worst thing that happened.

MARY. Well, the part I was here for –

JACKIE. (*eager*) Yes! You were here for some of it. So you know about –

MARY. Yes.

JACKIE. And I got to be honest it was hard when you left. I know you had to, if I could've, but I was so little, but I would've, how old were you when you –

MARY. Sixteen was when I went to boarding school and –

JACKIE. And you didn't come back and I don't blame you. If I could've, I would've too. You had relatives who could, I didn't, and I was so little, and she, I don't know why she couldn't...

MARY. She made a lot of bad choices, obviously.

JACKIE. Yes she did. She made some shitty fucking choices.

MARY. (*offended but trying*) I mean it was no picnic for me either. Obviously I had to go. But I was very alone. I wanted to come back. To at least visit. But that wasn't really an option.

JACKIE. No no I know I just... I wrote you letters. I don't know if she ever sent them.

MARY. No. She didn't.

JACKIE. She should've. Because I wanted, I really missed you. And after you were gone, Dad, –

MARY. You know what, Jackie. Jackie you know what? This is just, I can see how much this is upsetting you. And we don't have to do this.

JACKIE. No, I want –

MARY. I know. You want to be a family. And that's what I want too. But we don't have to do it all at once. We can be friends now. And little by little, get to know each other. That's what I'm hoping for. Here, do you mind? I didn't mean to leave this just lying around.

(*She steps forward to take the stamps.* **JACKIE** *stops her.*)

JACKIE. We uh, okay. Okay. We don't have to talk about, we don't, it's okay. But we do have to talk about the stamps. Because that guy today – you liked him, right?

MARY. Dennis? Charming. Now, that man is a philatelist.

JACKIE. He seems to be that, yes, and some other things too. And he had a thought. After we all had that nice visit, you know, talking about the stamps, and calling those stamp dealers, that was fun, and when I walked him to the door? He mentioned something about the stamps. About selling the stamps.

MARY. We've already discussed this.

JACKIE. We have to discuss it again, Mary. I know you don't want to. But it would solve everything. Free and clear, you and I would both be free and clear from all of it, all the past would go away if we sold the stamps. We could pay off everything, everything would be gone, and we would both have something –

MARY. I do have something. I have my inheritance. From my grandfather. The only father I had.

JACKIE. Mary – we're the family. You and I are the family, that's why Mom wanted you to come back so that –

MARY. Is that what this is about? You want to be a "family," I guess it's pretty clear what that means.

JACKIE. It means –

MARY. They warned me, you know. They did warn me about this.

JACKIE. They, they who?

MARY. Everybody. They said, don't come. I mean, I know you're angry because I wasn't here earlier, but I almost didn't come at all, because I was afraid, people told me to be afraid, that there was probably some sort of financial quagmire, that that's really what this was all about. Getting me here to help out with the financial quagmire. People said that! But I didn't believe them. I said, it's my mother and my sister, and I need to be there for them. It's not money! That's not why they're asking me! I told everyone that. And that's what I'm telling you. I came because I wanted to be here, to help you, and go to the funeral, and see her again, I really wanted that. But if what you're saying is that you had another motive, an ulterior financial motive? I am not a party to that. I wasn't even here! So. If there is a financial issue? It is not my responsibility. That is my position. Okay? Okay, Jackie?

(*Beat.*)

MARY. I'm sorry.

JACKIE. It's okay.

MARY. Can I get you anything? A glass of water?

JACKIE. (*beat*) A glass of water, would be great.

MARY. Good. I'm so glad we had this conversation. I feel a lot better.

(*She carefully takes the stamps, and goes.* **JACKIE** *looks at the papers again, then suddenly throws them across the room. They go flying. She takes a breath, reaches down to start picking them up again, sees a box, stands, and then kicks the box over. Things spill out. She glances into another box, then picks it up, turns it over and dumps it on the floor. Does it a third time.*

It is a real mess. After a moment, she reaches in a box, finds an old-fashioned cigarette pack holder, dumps out her dead mother's cigarettes, and puts one in her mouth. She finds a lighter in that box, lights the smoke, and pockets the lighter. She relaxes. After a moment, **MARY** *enters, with water and stamps.*)

MARY. (*continuing*) Oh, for heavens sake, what happened? What happened?

(*Surprised by the mess, she sets the stamps down as she steps into the room.* **JACKIE** *has her eye on them. Behind* **MARY**'s *back, she grabs them.*)

JACKIE. Nothing.

MARY. Well, something clearly –

(*appalled, sees the cigarette*)

I'm sorry. Are you smoking? Inside the house?

JACKIE. Want to have a conversation about it? I so enjoy our conversations.

(*She smokes, looks at the stamps.*)

MARY. Look. Could I have my stamps, please? It makes me really nervous to see you just –

JACKIE. Just what? Smoking? In front of the stamps? Why, because it's bad for them to know that I smoke?

MARY. All right, fine. I don't care what you do to your lungs. Just give me my stamps.

JACKIE. Fuck you. You come in here, this is so precious to me, those are my stamps, me and my fucking holy fucking grandfather, oh jewelry! You can have that Jackie! The only problem is it's not worth a FUCKING DIME.

MARY. I'm sorry, do you have to use language like that!

JACKIE. Yes, I fucking well think I do.

MARY. Okay. What you've gone through, both of us, but you especially, is upsetting and clearly, I think, you clearly need to take the time to calm down, and I will be upstairs, and give you the room to do that.

JACKIE. Calm down. That's not exactly what I was thinking of doing. More what I've been thinking about? Is finding some sort of plastic bag, you know, some sort of clear, strong plastic? And then I was thinking I'd figure out how to fasten that around your head, with some duct tape.

MARY. I'm sorry, but I'm beginning to think some real questions have to be raised about your character.

JACKIE. My CHARACTER? I have no character. What I have is two tiny tiny slips of paper, so small that they barely exist, and I'm going to take them, and I'm going to stab myself in the chest with a pair of really sharp scissors, and then I'm going to put those two tiny tiny slips of paper inside my body, right where my heart is supposed to be. And then I'm going to grow a pair of wings, big, blue and green scaly wings, not beautiful wings, BUG wings, the kind that move real fast. And then I'm going to go. Somewhere. Where they like tall girls, with bug wings. And then I'm going to lay in the sun and have a margarita.

MARY. Give me the stamps. Give them to me.

JACKIE. Yeah, I'll get right on that. 'Cause you know what I read today, on the internet? Something called the Three Skilling Banco got sold about ten years ago, for two and a half million dollars. The one cent magenta, some stamp from British Guiana which some zillion-aire has in some bank vault somewhere, they think that's worth maybe ten million dollars. Guess what else. Seven years ago a pair of uncanceled One and Two Penny Post Office stamps? Went for six million dollars. At auction. Can you believe that? Six. Million. Dollars.

MARY. Grandfather always said, they should be in a museum. But I had no idea –

JACKIE. Fuck museums.

MARY. You cannot say that. You can't – and you can't sell them. They're worth so much more than than mere money, they're –

JACKIE. "Mere" money? I'm sorry, what did you say did you say "mere" money did you actually say that?

MARY. I would like my stamps please.

JACKIE. You don't get it yet, but you will. Two little slips of paper. And I am born. "You're an interesting girl, Jackie." He has no idea.

(*She picks up the stamp book.*)

MARY. You are not walking out of this house with those stamps!

JACKIE. You know that trick, with the plastic bag and the duct tape? Want to know how I know about that?

MARY. I will call the police. I will –

JACKIE. You will what, you will tell them that I took your stamp collection? That'll make a big impression.

MARY. YES, YES, I will tell them – you stole my, my –

JACKIE. It's not yours –

MARY. It is mine –

(**MARY** *reaches for them, sudden.* **JACKIE** *throws a punch, gets her right across the face.* **MARY** *falls.* **JACKIE** *just looks at her, unmoved.*)

JACKIE. You come in here, you act like you know something, like you have rights, you don't know anything and you have no rights. You left. The fucking apocalypse fell on this family and YOU LEFT. And as a consequence I've earned these fucking stamps and I'm going to sell them. And if you think you're going to stop me? You'll lose.

(*She picks up the stamps and exits.*)

(*End of act one*)

ACT 2

(**PHILIP**'s *shop*. **JACKIE** *enters, carrying the book.*
DENNIS *is there, alone.*)

DENNIS. There you are! Come in, Jackie, come in! You're prompt!

JACKIE. Yes, Dennis, I am.

DENNIS. Good, good. You brought the stamps, good.

JACKIE. Yes.

DENNIS. Can I –

JACKIE. No, you can't. Sorry.

DENNIS. Of course, no, I understand completely. Can I get you something, Jackie? A beer, or –

JACKIE. A beer would be great, Dennis, thanks.

DENNIS. So my buyer's not here just yet, I sent him off with explicit instructions to liquefy every asset he possibly can, so that we can make this happen as quickly and as effortlessly as possible.

JACKIE. That's great, Dennis. Sounds like a plan.

DENNIS. Good. Here you go.

(*He hands her a beer. She toasts him with it.*)

JACKIE. Thanks.

(*They drink.*)

DENNIS. So let me give you a kind of run down of how I'm hoping this will work.

JACKIE. Okay.

DENNIS. You know, already, that I have somebody who might be interested in purchasing the one AND the two penny post office stamps. He wants both of them. That's what we're looking at here.

JACKIE. Yes, I'm aware of that.

DENNIS. So, he's going to be showing up – any minute, I presume – with a rather substantial amount of money, in cash, that he's willing to part with in exchange for your stamps.

JACKIE. Uh huh.

DENNIS. So I was thinking, maybe we, you and I, could take a minute, since we have a minute, to allude, or generalize even, in terms of what kind of a region we're talking about, in regards to the financial end of this discussion.

JACKIE. How much do I want for the stamps? Is that what you're asking?

DENNIS. Well, that would be the crass way of putting it.

JACKIE. Don't want to be crass.

DENNIS. I just meant that obviously what we want is to be in discussion.

JACKIE. I'm open to discussion. I love discussion.

DENNIS. Good. Good! You want some chips, Jackie?

JACKIE. No, I'm good, Dennis. So how much is he, your buyer I mean, bringing into this discussion?

DENNIS. I have no idea.

JACKIE. Well because that would be one way of starting the general area of discussion about the financial end. How much he actually has.

DENNIS. Another would be for you to talk about how much you're looking for.

JACKIE. Another would be, how much the stamps are worth on an open market.

DENNIS. What is an open market?

JACKIE. I could walk back out that door and find out.

(*Beat.*)

DENNIS. It's impossible of course to say how much those stamps are worth. On an open market? There's no such thing as an open market. I mean, you might read things, there's all sorts of crazy information out there about how much people have paid in similar situations, but that's obviously irrelevant.

JACKIE. Why obviously, Dennis?

DENNIS. Well, because – Jackie – I don't want to talk down to you –

JACKIE. I don't want that either, Dennis –

DENNIS. No no of course that would be not anything either of us was interested in. But, the fact is, commerce is always a complicated and nuanced arrangement.

JACKIE. Much of life is.

DENNIS. Absolutely. I couldn't agree with you more. But in this particular situation –

JACKIE. "Arrangement" I think is what you said a minute ago –

DENNIS. Yes, arrangement, that is better, the questions about the free hand of the marketplace beg a sophistication and specificity of analysis.

JACKIE. Wow, Dennis. That does sound pretty complicated. I mean, I thought we were just talking about selling some stamps.

(*Beat.*)

DENNIS. That is what we're talking about.

JACKIE. So what's the offer?

DENNIS. What do you want?

JACKIE. I want you to tell me how much this guy thinks he's gonna steal my stamps for.

DENNIS. Whoa, whoa, that's a –

JACKIE. Dennis. I went on line. I know what they're worth.

DENNIS. This is what I'm talking about. The wealth of shabby information, of misinformation which is careening out there on the internet is ludicrous. The hysteria of information, for that is what it is, hysteria –

JACKIE. So you're not hoping to steal them.

DENNIS. Absolutely not.

JACKIE. Dennis. I'm perfectly willing to have you steal these stamps. But you have to steal them for a price.

(*Beat*)

DENNIS. This is why it's useful. To have general, allusive conversations. About intent, and interest –

JACKIE. Dennis. Can we just cut this out for a second, and get to the point? How fucking interesting are these stamps, to you?

DENNIS. Not as interesting as you are.

JACKIE. Listen. I have conceded that you're going to steal the stamps. The question is, for how much? And I'm not conceding any more than that. So where are we now?

(*Beat*)

DENNIS. You want some chips?

JACKIE. No, I don't want any chips.

DENNIS. Another beer?

JACKIE. (*slight pause, slightly bright*) Yeah sure Dennis, how about another beer?

(*Beat. He doesn't move.*)

DENNIS. You haven't really touched the one you have.

JACKIE. No, I haven't.

DENNIS. Maybe we should wait, then.

JACKIE. Maybe we should.

(*Beat.*)

DENNIS. What kind of nonsense did you read on line?

JACKIE. What are you thinking you are going to steal them for?

DENNIS. Just say it.

JACKIE. You say it.

DENNIS. A hundred thousand.

JACKIE. Fuck you.

(*She stands and heads for the door.*)

DENNIS. WAIT. Wait, wait.

(*beat*)

A million.

(*beat*)

You want much more than that –

JACKIE. I know what they're worth, so yeah, I want more than that, and I can get it, too, fast –

DENNIS. We can go higher than that –

JACKIE. How much higher?

DENNIS. Higher.

JACKIE. (*sick of this*) How much higher, Dennis?

DENNIS. I don't know!

(*She heads for the door.*)

DENNIS. (*continuing; a little more urgent*) I told you, he's bringing cold cash into this, so I don't know how much higher than a million he can go. Come on. This is a negotiation! Come on, come on, you said yourself that you were willing to let me steal them. For a price. I mean, if that's where you're willing to start – you started there, Jackie, you said, steal for a price – so from my end you have to expect that I'm going to try to steal them for nothing! That's the only play available to me! Seriously, seriously, it's not personal. And it's certainly no reason to walk away. You said what you needed to say, and I did what I needed to do, and now I know that you're not going to let me do that, which is a good thing to know, a very good thing to understand about this situation, and each other. That's the way I'm looking at this, Jackie. I hope you are, too.

(*Beat.*)

JACKIE. So where is this guy?

DENNIS. Sterling? He's on his way.

JACKIE. Because this wasn't the deal. That I sit around and wait for him.

DENNIS. Trust me, he'll show up. Sterling is a highly motivated buyer. He's coming. With a big suitcase full of cash. I promise.

JACKIE. Sterling, what kind of name is Sterling anyway. What's his story?

DENNIS. What isn't his story? He's rich. He's a rich rich international businessman type of person. Named Sterling.

JACKIE. What kind of business?

DENNIS. Murky stuff. You know, real estate, corporate merger-type, governmental arms deals, that sort of thing.

JACKIE. He's an arms dealer?

DENNIS. He's a lot of things. I can never really keep track. Mostly we talk about stamps. He loves stamps, a lot.

JACKIE. You collect stamps, too?

DENNIS. Did. It can be a rather expensive hobby. As I think you learned from your road trip down the information freeway.

JACKIE. So what happened, you had money, and now you don't?

(DENNIS *thinks about this for a moment, and half-laughs, at himself, as he considers how to answer that question.*)

DENNIS. (*finally*) You know, Jackie, I'm actually not terribly interested in the past, what good is it, really, dwelling on the past?

JACKIE. I couldn't agree more.

DENNIS. Right? I mean, you know what they say about the stamps. It's the errors that make them valuable. That's kind of my theory on people.

JACKIE. (*a short laugh*) I like that theory.

DENNIS. Good. So what are you going to do with the money? I mean, a million bucks, more, I mean, more than a million, that'll buy a lot of comic books.

JACKIE. What?

DENNIS. You said, when you came in yesterday, you were in some store buying comic books. Didn't you say that?

JACKIE. (*defensive*) A comic book.

DENNIS. Yeah, okay, so which one?

JACKIE. You read comic books?

DENNIS. Everybody reads comic books. So what are you into?

(*A beat. She considers this question.*)

JACKIE. The one I just bought is called... Elfquest. It's kind of a classic, actually.

DENNIS. What's it about?

JACKIE. Well. There's this Troll, and he's got a spell that these Elves want? And this girl, to help them out – because she was raised by humans but that didn't work out so then these elves and these wolf people adopt her, so she wants to help them, because they, you know, she's part wolf and part elf and part human, she's the only one who can do it. And there's this wizard she has to, um... anyway...

(*Beat.*)

DENNIS. What does the wizard do?

JACKIE. He helps her. He, he's her friend, and he helps her.

(*beat*)

Look. Um, you know, if this guy doesn't get here soon, I'm taking off.

DENNIS. Don't do that.

JACKIE. (*uncomfortable now*) This doesn't feel right. I know what I got. I can easily find another buyer.

DENNIS. I know you can. But you don't have to. This could be so easy. You could just walk away with a lot of money, no questions asked. Sometimes life really is that easy.

JACKIE. Oh yes, I've so noticed.

DENNIS. (*stricken with a sudden bout of conscience*) Look. Sterling, he's a tricky guy. And when he wants something, that's both a good and a bad thing. He has, uh, shall we say, strong emotions, especially when – he wants something *strongly*. Which is why I think that maybe you should let me – .

JACKIE. Handle this delicate but easy negotiation.

DENNIS. Yes.

JACKIE. Because you're so honest. And I can trust you.

(*beat*)

I do trust you, Dennis. I trust you completely.

DENNIS. Shit.

JACKIE. Yeah.

(*The door opens.* **STERLING** *is there, with a suitcase.* **JACKIE** *turns and looks at him, involuntarily backs away.* **STERLING** *enters.*)

STERLING. Hey.

DENNIS. Sterling. Hi. Hi.

STERLING. Is that it?

DENNIS. Real nice. Sterling, I'd like to introduce you to Jackie, I've told you about Jackie, Jackie, this is Sterling.

JACKIE. Hello.

STERLING. I'd like to see it. Them. I'd like to see them.

JACKIE. I'd like to see how serious you are about buying them, Sterling. Open the suitcase. I want to see the cash.

(**STERLING** *looks at her, looks at* **DENNIS**, *laughs for a moment.*)

STERLING. Is she kidding?

DENNIS. I, I'm not sure.

STERLING. She wants to see my money? What does she think this is, some kind of drug deal?

JACKIE. Maybe you should ask me what I think, asshole.

STERLING. All right. What the fuck do you think this is? I should be asking you questions, you with all your claims of having found the holy grail of philately, I'm not asking, and I don't even know you, who are you, I am not asking you –

JACKIE. (*overlap, loud*) YEAH, IN FACT, YOU ARE ASKING ME. YOU ASKED ME QUITE CLEARLY TO SHOW YOU THE STAMPS. AND I AM SAYING QUITE CLEARLY BACK, I WILL SHOW YOU THE STAMPS WHEN YOU SHOW ME THE MONEY.

DENNIS. (*overlapping both*) Whoa, whoa, Jackie – now now now –

STERLING. What, you think this is some sort of fucking game show?

JACKIE. What I think is, I'm walking out that door if you don't open that suitcase and show me what kind of fool you think you're taking me for.

STERLING. This is a joke.

JACKIE. Wrong answer.

(*She starts for the door.*)

DENNIS. Jackie no no no, come on, Jackie, please, I've worked really hard to set this deal up I am so sorry that Sterling is high strung, I told you he was, I warned you, please don't – Jackie, come on, JACKIE –

(*She is halfway through the door.* DENNIS *grabs her.*)

STERLING. WAIT. I SAID WAIT.

(JACKIE *turns and looks at him.* STERLING *finally lifts the suitcase and puts it on the counter. He opens it. It is full of cash.* JACKIE *takes a half step back in, doesn't even glance at it, looks at* DENNIS, *shrugs.*)

JACKIE. Too late.

(*She goes.*)

DENNIS. Wait whoa whoa whoa – JACKIE –

STERLING. What the fuck is this?

(DENNIS *grabs* JACKIE *by the arm and drags her back in.*)

DENNIS. Hey. You listen to me. This isn't someone you can mess around with. I think I've been very clear about that.

JACKIE. Get your hands off me, or the deal is off.

DENNIS. Okay, sorry, didn't mean to intrude on your personal space I was just trying to make a point. Everybody's tense, everyone has a lot at stake here, that's understood. Who wants a beer?

STERLING. What I want is to see the fucking stamps. She wanted to see the money, I took care of that. Now I want to see the stamps.

JACKIE. It's going to cost you.

STERLING. What?

JACKIE. It costs ten thousand dollars to look at the stamps.

(*Beat.*)

STERLING. Dennis? Do you want to talk to your client?

DENNIS. You are my client, Sterling. This person is a crazy person who has a whole series of demented ideas about which the meaning of which I have suddenly no clue. Jackie –

JACKIE. That's how it works. It costs, to look at the stamps, to see if they are what in fact you know they are, you have to pay for that. That other guy, that's what he said, when I brought them here, he said it costs –

DENNIS. Philip? Philip is insane –

JACKIE. Then why are we here? Why did you have me bring them here?

STERLING. What did Philip say, what did he tell her?

DENNIS. It doesn't matter, he's insane.

STERLING. Where is he, anyway?

DENNIS. I don't know, I thought he was with you.

STERLING. You were with me.

DENNIS. Well, I don't know where he is.

JACKIE. That's not my problem. You said, bring the stamps here. And that guy, his rule is –

DENNIS. He's insane –

JACKIE. He's the one who knows stamps. That's why he sent me here, that other guy –

DENNIS. That other, the the the comic book guy?

JACKIE. YES. The comic book guy. Sent me here. To talk to him. And he said –

DENNIS. He wouldn't even look at your stamps –

JACKIE. Thousands of dollars. To look at the stamps. That's the rule. I didn't make up the rules. I'm just the person who holds the stamps. And if I decide to give them up, it will be on my terms. Now, you both need to know that I'm not a crazy person. I don't like you saying I'm crazy because the fact is I am the least crazy person you have ever met. Logic that you don't see is private for a reason, and that reason is potentially the smartest, least crazy thing possible in any given situation. So because of that I insist that there be rules here. You and I both know I took a big risk in coming, so that means I'm not exactly playing hard to get. But within that I have protections. Those protections are the rules. And you. You're the other protection. I'm not stupid.

DENNIS. I know you're not.

JACKIE. If there aren't any protections I am leaving now. Do I have protections or not?

(*Beat.*)

DENNIS. You have protections.

STERLING. What the fuck is this, Dennis?

DENNIS. I'm trying to uh – Jackie – feels –

STERLING. I don't give a shit about her feelings! I mean, I can walk. I can end this too.

JACKIE. So end it.

STERLING. I haven't even seen the fucking stamps!

JACKIE. Pay me ten thousand dollars and you will.

STERLING. I don't have to pay you one red cent. I own those stamps.

JACKIE. Not yet you don't.

STERLING. Dennis.

DENNIS. Pay her.

STERLING. You sure about that?

DENNIS. It's movement, Sterling. To be philosophical, and I see no reason not to at times like this, when the river stops flowing, all the fish die. You give her the money, or we got a dead fish.

STERLING. If this goes south, she's not the only one taking the consequences on that.

DENNIS. Nothing is going south, just give her the money! You can pay her now or pay her later, the money's all going in the same direction, Sterling. It's fine. Just give it to her.

(**STERLING** *looks at him, turns, opens the suitcase, takes out a packet of bills and puts it on the counter. He shuts the suitcase, and turns, looks at her.* **JACKIE** *reaches for it. At the last minute,* **DENNIS** *stops her.*)

DENNIS. (*continuing*) Jackie, could I speak with you for a minute?

(*He takes her by the arm, leads her across the room. She shoves him, shrugging him off.*)

DENNIS. (*continuing*) On the subject of rules. You do understand that taking that money commits you. Do you understand that?

JACKIE. My understanding is just what I said it was, he has to pay, to look at my stamps.

DENNIS. Yes, and he has paid, and if you so much as lay a finger on that man's money it will be implicitly understood by everyone in this room that wherever this deal goes is irrelevant to the fact that it is going to make. These are the cold hard facts of commerce. Touching another person's money commits you. There is no backing out or changing your mind after that. Do you understand that?

JACKIE. Worried, Dennis?

DENNIS. You know, Jackie, yes in fact I am. This man is a serious collector and he has serious money and I can get him to give you a lot of that money for those stamps, I can do that for you, but we're entering rather nerve-wracking territory as far as I'm concerned and I really need to hear from you that you also understand the rules, the big rules, of a situation like this. The exchange of cash commits us all.

(*She looks at him, goes to the counter, looks at the money, picks it up, and puts it in her jacket. She then takes the stamp book, opens it and pushes it across the counter to* **STERLING**.)

STERLING. My god.

(*He looks at the stamps.* JACKIE *watches him, alert. He is in the throes of something quite unguarded and powerful. He reaches out to touch them.* JACKIE *reaches over to stop him.*)

JACKIE. Hang on, Sterling. I didn't say –

(DENNIS *suddenly and swiftly grabs her from behind, pulling her away from* STERLING.)

JACKIE. (*continuing; frightened*) Hey. Hey! Hey – no – no –

DENNIS. (*overlap*) Let him touch them. Let him touch them. Jackie. He needs to touch them.

JACKIE. LET GO OF ME.

(*He releases her, but she is struggling so wildly she falls to the floor. She turns and looks at him, really unnerved and furious.* STERLING *looks at* DENNIS, *then at* JACKIE, *unperturbed by the disturbance.*)

STERLING. (*to* JACKIE) You better not be messing with me. These are real?

JACKIE. Yeah, they're real.

STERLING. How'd you end up with them?

JACKIE. My mother died. They were in her stuff.

STERLING. And?

JACKIE. And what?

STERLING. Don't use that tone with me. If this checks out, I'm going to give you a lot of money for those stamps, and I got the right to ask questions. So where's Philip? He knew this was the time, yeah? So where is he? That's what I want to know, Dennis. I don't like it, he's not here.

DENNIS. It's his place; he has to show up eventually.

STERLING. So where did he go? Why did he leave?

DENNIS. I don't know.

STERLING. (*on the stamps*) Unbelievable. A one penny and a two penny. Together. Unbelievable.

(*He stares at the stamps, reaches out to touch them again.*)

JACKIE. I don't want you touching them. They're still my stamps.

STERLING. Hey. They are not your stamps. They are my stamps. There are a few remaining questions involved in this transition, but no one is in doubt about who those stamps belong to. Isn't that right, Dennis?

DENNIS. The remaining questions are rather large, but I'm not going to argue with your basic proposition.

STERLING. He talks well, doesn't he? That's one of the things I like about him. I could use a smoke, I feel like smoking. There's something post-coital about moments like this, but I don't want to get ahead of myself. Where the fuck is Philip? Fuck him, he doesn't get here in time to put in his two cents, he's just fucked. He's a moron, he doesn't want to be a part of this. Those stamps are phenomenal. Exquisite, right? Exquisite.

DENNIS. Yeah, well, as far as Phil goes, if you're happy –

STERLING. I'm not happy, I'm something else. Fuck yes I'm happy, those stamps are – where'd you find them? Don't tell me I don't want to hear that idiotic story about your dead mother again. Jesus, those are gorgeous stamps. Those stamps aren't out there. Both of them? Uncanceled? They aren't out there. How much does she want for them? No. Don't tell me. I want to hear it from her. You been giving me a lot of trouble tonight, what's your name, Jackie? Jackie, answer me. Is that your name?

JACKIE. Yes.

STERLING. It's all been very irritating and I understand that that was your purpose. You know you have something valuable, and you want to make sure I understand that this deal isn't going to be easy to make. You want me off my game, you want to keep me emotional, and you've been very successful so far in that endeavor. I respect that, Jackie, it's a tactic I've used plenty of times myself and I would not have suspected someone as young as you would have such command over this kind of territory. You surprised me, and I don't mind telling you I am not often surprised. Have a seat.

JACKIE. I'd rather stand.

STERLING. Whatever makes you happy. I don't want to piss you off here. I don't mind telling you, I don't like you when you're pissed. I, however, will sit.

(*he does*)

Okay, now you and I are going to talk about what you think you want, from me, as a fair price for those stamps.

DENNIS. Jackie and I have already had the beginnings of a discussion about this, Sterling –

STERLING. Dennis. As I said, I often enjoy listening to you talk, but this needs to be between me and Jackie. What do you want, Jackie? What do you want for those stamps?

JACKIE. You tell me.

(**STERLING** *considers this, smiles.*)

STERLING. You know what Dennis here said about you, when he brought your situation to me? He said, this girl is a lamb. And don't get me wrong, I like Dennis, but he was mistaken when he characterized you that way.

JACKIE. Yes he was.

STERLING. You know what else he said? He said you were damaged. So am I. Neither one of us is a lamb. Now, you don't want to name a figure. That's a good beginning. You make me name the price and then we go up instead of down. But I'll tell you, I'm not going to name a figure, either. What I will do for you is give you the beginning and the end. There are some times in life when everything is about negotiation. What I want, what you want, what Dennis wants, Philip, who knows what he wants or even where the fuck he is, all of that comes into play and then the ending is in question, because the negotiation isn't about the ending, that's why so many questions arise. Are you following this? Don't answer; I can see you are. You and I both know, this isn't about negotiation. You want money, and I want those stamps. Obviously there's more to it than that or you wouldn't be working my nerves the way you've been. You did some research, you found out how much those stamps may be worth?

JACKIE. Yes. I did.

STERLING. Good. I'd be embarrassed for you if you hadn't done that. Now I want to explain a few things about commerce, at this level of investment. Stamps like this, they are an investment to people, not a lot of people can afford to shell out several millions of dollars to own a One Penny and a Two Penny Post Office, but people who can, people to whom something like that might make sense? These stamps are an investment. In a different, more formalized situation, you go through a broker, you hire a couple of experts to authenticate the investment, you pay rather considerable taxes, state, local, federal, you need lawyers, accountants, trust me, no one is going to let you get through a multi-million dollar investment purchase without overhead that many many people consider onerous. Twenty five percent off the top, and that is not off the top of my end, that's out of your end. So one or two of your many millions has just been lopped off. At the outset.

In addition I hope you don't mind my pointing out – you like rules, I heard you mention to Dennis, before, that rules you see as being protections, you're aware of the need for protections? Jackie, you get more formalized, in the hope of gathering to yourself more money in exchange for your valuable product here, and the rules become your enemy. And what I've seen of you, Jackie – neither one of us is particularly at home in situations where there's a lot of fools to suffer. Where a lot of noise enters the equation. Where the the intimacy is lost. Because what we're talking about here, Jackie – what is going on between you and me – is a most intimate exchange. People want to lie about that, confuse that, but they are liars and they are obfuscators. You have time for that? Months, years, to waste on a lot of people wanting to participate, to interfere, to degrade what you and I are doing here? Because I don't have months to waste. I don't even have days. I know what I want out of life. And this is it.

(*He stands, goes to the stamps.*)

STERLING. (*continuing*) Now. This is my understanding of what it is you want. You want money, yes, that is the primary reason you took the chances you did, to come here tonight. But you want more than that. You want respect, and you want recognition for your courage and your determination. Now. I give you that. Yes?

JACKIE. Yes.

STERLING. Yes. And I give you this, too.

(*He gets the suitcase from behind the counter, brings it out front, and opens it. He gestures to her, to come forward. She does.*)

STERLING. (*continuing*) I want you to count it. And decide. The beginning, and the end. No negotiation. This is what I brought here, to make this happen tonight. It is a shitload of money. It is more money than you ever in your wildest dreams imagined having, at any one point in your young life. Is it what those stamps are worth? Who's to say?

It is cash, it is under the table, there's no overhead, there's no lawyers, there's no fucking accountants here, to drive you and me fucking crazy with their nonsense. That's added value; you can't deny it. You also can't deny that at this moment? Those stamps are only worth what I will pay for them. In the future, if you took a chance, could you get more for them, from someone else? Maybe. But I don't live in the future. I live in the present. In my world, the present is the only moment that exists. And this is the only deal that exists. That amount of money. For those two stamps.

(*He steps away, a gentleman, gestures to the money.*)

Please.

(*She looks at him, looks at* **DENNIS**, *steps forward and touches the money. She shudders a bit, grips the side of the suitcase, then reaches in and takes out several bundles. She counts. It takes quite a long time. She is really pretty thorough. She looks up at* **STERLING**, *then back to* **DENNIS**.)

JACKIE. How much of this goes to him?

STERLING. None.

DENNIS. Really?

STERLING. Not one red cent. Dennis and I know each other, he and I will come to an agreement apart from my arrangement with you. That's none of your concern. This amount is the top end of what I was willing to pay for those stamps. I hoped, frankly, as a businessman I don't mind admitting that I hoped not to have to go this high. But I don't want to waste your time. That is as high as I'm willing to go.

(*She looks at him.*)

JACKIE. That's it?

STERLING. That's it. That's the deal.

(*She considers him, then, after a moment, goes to the stamps, closes the book and picks it up. She turns back and looks at him. He looks at her. He smiles. She smiles. He nods, enjoying this suddenly.*)

STERLING. (*continuing*) Yeah, okay. Okay.

(*He reaches into his jacket and takes out another packet of money, which he drops into the open suitcase. She looks at him, smiling. He takes out a second packet, and then a third, which he drops into the suitcase.*)

STERLING. (*continuing*) That's it.

JACKIE. Thank you.

(*He closes the suitcase and hands it to her. She takes it and hands him the stamps.*)

STERLING. Thank you. I like her, Dennis. She's not a fool. You want to come have a drink with me, young lady?

JACKIE. No thank you.

STERLING. Perhaps another time.

> (*He goes. After a moment,* **JACKIE** *looks at* **DENNIS**. *She screams, happy. He grabs her and swings her around, both of them laughing with great excitement. Finally he sets her down. They consider each other, happy, and perhaps about to kiss, when the door opens.* **PHILIP** *is there.*)

DENNIS. Hey, Phil, where you been? You missed all the action.

> (*But the door swings open a second time.* **STERLING** *enters. His mood is decidedly different.*)

DENNIS. (*continuing*) What?

> (*The door swings open a third time.* **MARY** *enters. She is nervous, timid.*)

STERLING. (*cold, but for the moment, calm*) What's going on here, Dennis?

DENNIS. Nothing.

JACKIE. She – she has *nothing* to say about this.

MARY. Oh, I have a great deal to say about this.

> (**STERLING** *hands* **PHILIP** *the stamps.* **PHILIP** *takes the book to the counter.*)

JACKIE. No, you don't.

> (*to* **STERLING**)

> She doesn't, she knows nothing.

STERLING. Is that so?

> (**PHILIP** *has opened the book.* **MARY** *goes to him, watching as he looks at the stamps.*)

JACKIE. I'm not kidding. What has she been telling you, some insane story about the stamps, they're her stamps, she has some claim, it's nonsense. I don't even know her. She has no claim.

MARY. That is a lie.

JACKIE. It's not a lie!

STERLING. Dennis?

DENNIS. I don't think it's anything you need to worry about, Sterling. I really don't. It doesn't change anything as far as you're concerned.

STERLING. Is that so? Philip?

PHILIP. She's telling the truth. They're her stamps.

JACKIE. They are not her stamps.

(PHILIP *reaches into the counter, takes out an eyepiece and continues to study the stamps.*)

STERLING. She's telling the truth?

JACKIE. She's not telling the truth, she wouldn't know the truth if it fell on her head! She's a complete lunatic who I happen to be vaguely related to, that is as much as you can say about this demented woman! I don't even know what she's doing here!

MARY. You know –

JACKIE. Oh my god, I swear to you, Mary, if you fuck this up I will fucking kill you!

DENNIS. Jackie –

MARY. (*wounded, to* PHILIP *and* STERLING) I promise you. I never intended for any of this to happen. I told her, that she shouldn't do this, I told her, it would be wrong.

JACKIE. You don't get to say what's wrong! They are not your stamps. They are not her stamps!

PHILIP. It doesn't matter whose stamps they are. They're not real. They're fakes.

(DENNIS *looks at him, looks at* STERLING.)

DENNIS. They're not. Come on. They're not. I looked at them myself. So did Sterling. We don't know nothing, between us. Those stamps are real.

MARY. They're not.

(*Beat.*)

JACKIE. You are such a liar. You told me yourself, they're worth millions. You told me. They're the crown jewel of, of...

MARY. (*embarrassed*) Grandfather thought they were. For a while. He, he bought them from someone in Switzerland, when he was on a business trip over there and he was so pleased with himself. For several years. And then he, he felt that he needed to have his entire collection, um, you know, expertised, for insurance, he wanted to insure it so he had an expert look at everything and, and – they were fakes. He was devastated.

JACKIE. That's nuts. You said –

MARY. I know what I said.

PHILIP. They're very good fakes. But they're fakes. You can particularly see it on the one penny, the ink started to discolor, it's running to yellow along the left border. And there's a muddiness on both "e's", it looks like there was ink removed and then etching repairs made on both stamps. I'm not sure how they did it; they may have gotten hold of a more common stamp, probably the forty eight? That's the theory on the magenta forgery, somebody doctored a four cent, made it look like a one cent. Whatever it was, these are fakes.

JACKIE. No. Come on.

DENNIS. (*growing desperation*) Come on. There's controversy, around these things. The magenta forgery, so-called, people still can't agree about that. Dempsey says yes, that guy in Sweden says no –

PHILIP. Lagerloef?

DENNIS. A lot of people think that magenta is authentic, you know that. The missionary stamps, everybody thought those were forgeries –

PHILIP. The missionary stamps ARE forgeries –

DENNIS. (*overlap*) They're not! They verified that those cancellation marks were historically accurate –

PHILIP. (*overlap*) Whether or not the missionary stamps are forgeries will remain a controversy for years. This however will not.

DENNIS. Come on, look at the – that line, where the ink is discolored, that's not because it's a fake, that's from an earlier mount. You can see, it's just lost a little glue, that's a mark from an earlier mount. Come on. We need to get another opinion, Sterling. Sterling, listen to me. It is utterly impossible that those stamps are fakes.

STERLING. Impossible? Really. How so, Dennis? Really, how so?

DENNIS. It just is. We'll talk to, we'll go to London.

STERLING. I am not going to London! I warned you about this. Did I not warn you?

DENNIS. (*handling him, fast*) Yes, you did, Sterling, you did, and listen, I don't believe it? I do not for one moment believe him, not without a second or even a third opinion, but if it does turn out to be what she is now claiming, I obviously did not know. It was my idea to ask Phil to to authenticate the stamps, why would I do that if I were trying to con you? You were the one who said fuck him when he wasn't here, you believed the way I did, both of us trusted our our innate knowledge. About what we saw. I still trust it.

STERLING. Do you, Dennis?

DENNIS. Yes.

JACKIE. Look. That stamp is real. She told me. She told me everything about it. The crown jewel, Mauritius, FDR –

MARY. That's – that's actually why he couldn't sell it to FDR. Because it wasn't real. He didn't want anyone else to know. But he knew. And that's why, he couldn't do it. And that's why I couldn't tell. It wasn't my secret to tell.

(*Beat.*)

STERLING. Philip. You're sure.

PHILIP. I'm sure. Of course I'm sure. He put together a first rate con and you fell for it.

DENNIS. I did not – I did not know –

PHILIP. (*with growing delight*) No, you're right, you're right! You didn't know. Neither did he. Both of you fell, hook line and sinker. And you didn't wait. Did you? Why wait for Philip, the Holy Grail was in front of you and you were so sure of what you knew, you looked at those stamps and you told yourself, they're real, didn't you, Sterling, you told yourself I don't need *Philip*, I know what's real and what's fake, I'll spend – what'd you spend? Don't tell me, it doesn't matter. However high you went it was too fucking high, because those stamps are worthless, and this girl conned you, whether she meant to or not, you wanted it and so you told yourself it was real, you conned yourself, you fucking loser. You think you know something about stamps, Sterling? You don't know shit.

JACKIE. That's not what happened.

STERLING. You shut up.

JACKIE. I didn't –

STERLING. I said, shut up.

(*He backhands her across the face. There is a shocked pause. She looks at him, then, fearless, spits at him. He grabs her by the throat.*)

DENNIS. Oh fuck.

(*She digs her nails into his arms and then twists, biting his hand. Enraged now, he slings her behind the counter, sending* **PHILIP** *and the others in the opposite direction.*)

DENNIS. (*overlap*) Sterling, stop it! Sterling – Jesus Christ, Sterling, she didn't know, nobody knew, Sterling –

MARY. (*overlap*) Oh my god oh my god, somebody do something!

PHILIP. No. Stop this. Stop it. I will not have this in my shop.

STERLING. Get the fuck up!

JACKIE. (*fighting him*) Fuck you, you mother fucking piece of shit!

(*He starts to strangle her.*)

DENNIS. Sterling, you're going to kill her Sterling! Sterling do not kill her! There are witnesses here! This is not something you can walk away from unless you stop right now. You kill her, and you are not going to walk away.

(**STERLING** *stops. He drops* **JACKIE** *to the floor, then puts his hands up.*)

STERLING. Sorry.

(*He steps over* **JACKIE** *and goes to pick up his suitcase. He looks back at* **PHILIP**, *then changes his mind and goes back to* **JACKIE**. *He goes through her jacket pockets until he finds the money. He tosses it on the counter.*)

STERLING. (*continuing*) There you go, Phil. There's your fee. Dennis. You'll hear from me about this.

(*He gets the suitcase and heads for the door.*)

PHILIP. Don't come back.

(**STERLING** *looks at him, laughs, and goes.* **DENNIS** *goes to* **JACKIE**.)

DENNIS. Jackie? You okay, Jackie? Phil, get me a wet washrag, would you?

JACKIE. I'm fine. It's old territory. I'm fine.

(*He helps her stand. She pushes him away.*)

JACKIE. (*continuing*) And you know, thanks for all the help, Mary. You'd kept your mouth shut? We could've all had a real nice dinner tonight. In Paris.

MARY. It would not have been right.

JACKIE. Yes, what just happened was clearly a much better plan. I'm so grateful your conscience saved us all.

MARY. They were not your stamps, to sell.

JACKIE. They apparently weren't ANYONE'S stamps to sell, Mary. You might have mentioned that when I asked you about them.

DENNIS. Jackie, come on. You need to let someone look at –

JACKIE. (*cutting him off*) I got hit in the face, Dennis. It will undoubtedly bruise up, and then I'll get a black eye. Is this news?

DENNIS. Apparently not.

JACKIE. No. It's not.

(*She goes to the counter, exhausted, picks up the stamps and turns toward the door.*)

PHILIP. What are you, what are you doing?

JACKIE. I'm going home, isn't that –

(*She stops, looks at him.*)

JACKIE. (*continuing; a short laugh*) What do you mean, what am I doing?

PHILIP. Nothing.

(*She looks at him for a moment, then looks at* **MARY**. *Something uncomfortable grows in the moment.*)

JACKIE. Okay. Yeah, okay. Listen. I just need to ask – how did you two even find each other?

PHILIP. I was looking for you. I called my friend. The guy who sent you here.

JACKIE. The comic book guy.

PHILIP. He had you on a mailing list.

JACKIE. Yeah. Yeah, that's clever, that's, but you know, that still doesn't –

PHILIP. I wanted to see the stamps.

(*A beat.*)

DENNIS. She was bringing them here. I told you, Philip. She was bringing them here.

PHILIP. I wasn't sure she'd show up.

DENNIS. I told you –

PHILIP. You're not the most reliable soul on the planet, Dennis! And I wanted to see the stamps! And it was a good thing I did, because –

DENNIS. Because what, because you were able to come back in time to save Sterling's ass, stop him from spending all his hard-earned money on stamps that are basically worthless? You hate Sterling –

PHILIP. That's beside the point.

DENNIS. Is it?

MARY. They weren't her stamps to sell. That's the point. It is! They were not your stamps to sell.

JACKIE. You said that already.

MARY. Well, I'm sorry, but it's simply true, and I would like you to give them back to me. *Please.*

JACKIE. (*thinking about this*) You know, Mary – I was telling Dennis, before, about this comic book I read. I bought it from this store, this comic book store, where the guy told me, I asked this guy, he's really nice, so I ASKED HIM about the stamps, and he said you should go talk to my friend Philip, who's a real expert this guy, this guy, Philip, loves stamps! He's a world class, he's this person, who who – *knows*. Stamps. And –

(*starting to put it all together, truly*)

– oh, boy – and you know, that guy in the comic book store, he's always so nice to me. Always, kind of, through all of it, so, I thought, you know… I thought… I made a mistake. Didn't I?

MARY. I am tired of listening to you prattle on about I don't know what.

JACKIE. What did he tell you? Our little stamp guy here, who knows everything. When he came to the house. What did he say, that he'd get them back for you, if you told this preposterous story about insurance and having the stamps, what did you call it, "expertised?"

DENNIS. You're a piece of shit, Philip.

PHILIP. You asked me to be here, to authenticate the stamps, that's what I did! You don't like it, you don't like the truth? You and Sterling were stupid together? You thought this was your big score? You were wrong. Now, get out of my shop. And don't come back. I'm sick to death of you.

DENNIS. I'll go. You bet I'll go. Come on, Jackie, let's go. He's full of shit, he doesn't know anything, I want to get another opinion on these stamps.

(*He takes her by the arm and she goes with him. Before they can make it out the door.*)

MARY. Those are my stamps, you're not taking them anywhere!

DENNIS. You know what? You're right, they are your stamps. Here. You loved your grandfather, it was important to you to have his stamp collection, sentimental value, I totally get that. So here, you keep the collection, while Jackie and I go get these other two stamps "expertised."

(*He opens the book, rips out the page with the two stamps on it, hands it to* **JACKIE**, *and holds the book of stamps out to* **MARY**. **MARY** *just stands there.*)

DENNIS. (*continuing*) You don't want the collection? You'd rather have the two stamps? But these two stamps are WORTHLESS, according to him.

PHILIP. They are worthless. But they're still her stamps.

MARY. Yes. They're still my stamps.

DENNIS. (*turning on him*) Wow. That's really quite a trick, Phil. You say it, and then she says it. Impressive.

MARY. Give me my stamps.

PHILIP. Give her the stamps.

DENNIS. Wow, and it goes both ways.

MARY. Give me my stamps.

JACKIE. (*holding up the page of stamps*) Mary. I'm not mad. Well. I'm a little mad. You and the stamp guy wanted them for yourselves. And that's why you did it. Isn't that why you did it?

MARY. They weren't yours. Ever. In any sense. You didn't understand the value, the intrinsic spiritual value of something like that. I don't blame you, you clearly haven't had the opportunity to develop an appreciation for for something as elegant and precious and *timeless* as that stamp collection. I know what things must have been like for you all those years.

JACKIE. You don't, actually. I was going to tell you. But you don't have the right to know.

MARY. Well, you had no right to steal my stamps. And sell them to some *crook*.

JACKIE. I liked that crook. Until we tried to fuck him over, he was really pretty nice to me.

MARY. Well you are not going to have another opportunity to sell them to someone like that. Philip is contacting several philatelic museums on my behalf.

DENNIS. You going to just donate them to a museum? You're going to just give them away?

PHILIP. (*a catch*) Well, obviously, you wouldn't just – they're very valuable stamps, many museums would pay a great deal of money to –

DENNIS. Of course, of course!

MARY. This is a great opportunity for, for grandfather's work, his accomplishment, to be known in the wider community! FDR's stamp collection was broken up after he died, a lot of people consider that a real tragedy. That is not going to happen here.

DENNIS. I got to hand it to you, that is such a spectacular line of bullshit, Philip. That is so, so clever.

PHILIP. Those stamps belong to the world!

DENNIS. This isn't about the world! It's about a *score*. We had a score, Phil. A big one, you and me and her. And all of us needed it, and you fucked it up because you couldn't get over some fucking thing that happened with you and Sterling I don't even know when, years, YEARS, what the fuck was it that was so irredeemably irredeemable that you couldn't take tens of thousands of dollars from that man, you had to fuck this up because of something – don't even tell me. I don't want to know. I'm not interested in the past! It doesn't exist, you fucking moron! You live in a fog of something that doesn't exist and that's why you are, and why you will remain a lost man.

PHILIP. (*cold*) During her rule, Queen Victoria oversaw the glorious rise of industrial development and the triumph of the imperial market in even undiscovered corners of this vast and unknowable globe. But the British never misunderstood one simple truth, that meaning and value cannot be commodified. Those stamps are and have always been beyond your power. They are bigger than you. They are more hungry than you. They mean more than your life ever will mean. Two tiny slips of paper, with the face of an empire on them. The history behind that. Is more significant than anything your flesh will ever amount to.

DENNIS. Yeah. Thanks for sharing.

(*He goes after* **PHILIP**, *tries to strangle him.* **PHILIP** *hits him.* **MARY** *reacts, as they fight.*)

MARY. Oh, stop! Please, please, this is terrible, you have to stop this. Stop!

(*While they fight,* **JACKIE** *watches for a moment, then takes her lighter out of her pocket. She starts to light the page of stamps on fire.* **MARY** *turns and sees her.*)

MARY. (*continuing*) No. Jackie! She's burning the stamps!

(*They all turn and see* **JACKIE** *holding the lighter up to the page of stamps.*)

DENNIS. (*overlap*) Oh, no. No no no – Oh, fuck. Fuck. FUCK. Jackie, Jackie now –

PHILIP. Don't. My god. Don't, please please please please –

JACKIE. Back away. BACK AWAY.

(*They do.*)

Huh.

(*She flicks the lighter off.*)

PHILIP. Oh, my god. We should have let him kill you.

JACKIE. Yeah, maybe you should've.

DENNIS. Jackie, can I talk to you for a moment?

JACKIE. I think we're all pretty much past talking, Dennis.

DENNIS. Not talking I didn't mean talking I meant – reviewing. History, capitalism, Queen Victoria – Phil, help me out here – the vast –

PHILIP. – Unknowable globe.

(*She flicks the lighter on.*)

DENNIS. Please don't burn the stamps, Jackie. People have been behaving poorly, with regard to the stamps, I think that's true – Phil –

PHILIP. What?

DENNIS. You've behaved rather poorly, PHIL.

PHILIP. I'm sorry. I'm really sorry.

DENNIS. So there's remorse here. Definitely remorse, Jackie.

(*She flicks the lighter off.*)

DENNIS. (*continuing*) And you need to take that in –

(**JACKIE** *flicks the lighter on again, right next to the page. The others scream and* **DENNIS** *takes another step back.*)

– and and ask yourself – at times like this I think it's good to check in with you know, your own personal level of reactivity and your goals. Put reactivity aside, and ask yourself, what are the goals of a situation like this? What do you want?

(**JACKIE** *hears this; unflicks the lighter. She looks down at the stamps in her hand.*)

JACKIE. I just wanted something, for once, just something. Mary. There was enough for both of us. More than enough. You couldn't let me have anything? Not anything?

MARY. He wasn't your grandfather.

JACKIE. We could still sell them. You and me. If you just gave me something.

MARY. Why should I?

DENNIS. Again, the issue of goals here, Mary.

MARY. Those are my stamps. This is my inheritance. My property. Those were my – my – my grandfather – his heritage – he – and it's mine. And you're just, everything about you, you're a thief, you're a criminal. I won't let you blackmail me. I won't reward you! Why should you get anything? Go ahead. Burn them! Burn them! I won't give you anything!

(*There is a terrible moment as the two sisters consider each other.* **JACKIE** *drops the stamps to the floor, and turns away.* **PHILIP** *darts forward, grabs the stamps.*)

PHILIP. Thank god. Thank god. They're fine.

MARY. Oh my god. Are they all right?

PHILIP. Yes, they're fine. They're fine.

(*He hands them to her.* **MARY** *looks at them, then at* **JACKIE**.)

MARY. Jackie, I'm sorry. I wanted to be a good sister to you. Obviously I would be well within my rights to call the authorities and prosecute. But out of respect for our mother, I'm not going to do that.

(*beat*)

Don't you have anything to say to me?

JACKIE. Like what?

MARY. "Thank you?" Never mind.

(*to* **PHILIP**)

We need to get these someplace safe, immediately. Do you...

PHILIP. Yes yes, in the back I have a wall safe. Of course I do. It's been a long time since I had anything that really warranted it. But this... this is a great honor. This is a great day for me. I want you to know that from now on, everything will be done to esteem and protect these stamps. They are a great treasure.

JACKIE. Yes, they are.

PHILIP. The rest of them too, the whole collection.

(**DENNIS**, *at the counter, picks it up and hands it to* **MARY**, *who then scurries back to* **PHILIP**'s *side.*)

PHILIP. (*continuing*) We have a lot to talk about, but first these need to be secured.

(*back to* **DENNIS**)

When we return, I don't expect to see either one of you. She may have reservations about calling the authorities. I, however, do not. It would give me great pleasure to do it.

DENNIS. Fuck you, you fucking asshole.

PHILIP. It will take all of three minutes to do this. If you're still here? I'm making that call.

(*He takes* **MARY** *off, with the stamps.* **DENNIS** *looks at* **JACKIE**, *looks away, then –*)

DENNIS. That Philip is a total piece of shit. I mean, I did not have to include him. I included him as a favor and he fucked me royally. Fuck him. I truly wish for him all the misery that he is destined to bring down upon his own head; truly, I truly do.

(*then*)

For a second there, I really thought you were going to do it.

JACKIE. For a second there, I really was.

DENNIS. I don't blame you. That sister, wow! What a dim bulb. What a nitwit. You want, I know a lawyer, very good, we could sue her, tangle this whole thing up in the courts for so long, she'll be paying you just to get rid of the guy. This guy is very good.

JACKIE. No. It's better this way. No bug wings. No margaritas. No beaches in the middle of the Indian Ocean. And maybe that's the way things are supposed to be. Maybe too many things went wrong, before, when there wasn't any sense you could do anything about it. Or maybe someone did a terrible thing, that had to happen? There was nothing else to do? But maybe sometimes that's just the end of everything. Maybe to want to come back to life, maybe that's just – a curse.

(*She sits very still, lost.* **DENNIS** *goes to her.*)

DENNIS. Listen to me. Jackie? Listen to me. You're in shock.

JACKIE. Or maybe what I just said is just true.

DENNIS. No no no. The only thing that's true, really? Is you and I got fucked, which is unpleasant under any circumstances. It is also true that both of us kind of need to skip town for a little while. Nevertheless, both of us still have options. I have options; you have options.

(*He reaches into his pocket and holds something up.*)

You also have an inverted Jenny.

(*She looks at him surprised, looks back at where* **MARY** *and* **PHILIP** *have exited, then –*)

JACKIE. When did you do that?

DENNIS. Just now. It was hinged, couldn'tve been easier to lift. Anyway, it's not a post office. But it is still worth a lot of money.

JACKIE. Yeah, you told me. Three thousand dollars.

DENNIS. Did I say that? I may have lied.

JACKIE. You lied?

DENNIS. I may have. A little.

(*beat*)

Or, I may have lied a lot.

(*He helps her up, looking over her shoulder to see where* **PHILIP** *and* **MARY** *are.*)

It's the errors that make 'em valuable. An upside down plane? That's a big error.

JACKIE. (*beat*) So what's it worth?

DENNIS. Let's go talk about it. Let me buy you a margarita. On a beach. In Mexico.

(*He smiles at her, gestures to the door. Blackout.*)

(*End of play.*)

Also by
Theresa Rebeck...

Abstract Expression

Bad Dates

The Bells

The Butterfly Collection

Does This Woman Have a Name?

The Family of Mann

Loose Knit

Omnium Gatherum

The Scene

Spike Heels

Sunday on the Rocks

View of the Dome

The Water's Edge

CPSIA information can be obtained at www.ICGtesting.com
Printed in the USA
BVOW11s2012050114

340848BV00008B/134/P

9 780573 660191